The Wonderful Journey

written and illustrated by

Gill McBarnet

Ruwanga Trading

Also published by Ruwanga Trading Inc.:
The Whale Who Wanted to Be Small
A Whale's Tale
The Shark Who Learned a Lesson
The Goodnight Gecko
Gecko Hide and Seek
The Brave Little Turtle
The Gift of Aloha
Tikki Turtle's Quest

First published in 1986 by Ruwanga Trading:
ISBN 0-9615102-2-6
Printed in China through Everbest Printing Co., Ltd.

BOOK ENQUIRIES AND ORDERS:
Booklines Hawaii, Ltd.
269 Pali'i
Mililani, Hawaii 96789
Phone: (808) 676-0116
E-mail: bookline@lava.net

For Terry

All winter long Kanani the baby whale played with her friends in the warm waters of the reef. She played hide and seek with the striped scorpion fish, the golden trumpet fish and the parrot fish. The spotted eel often hid in the coral near the prickly sea urchin, but the shy little hermit crab had the best hiding place of all . . . inside his shell!

Days went into weeks and weeks into months and one day Kanani's mother said to her

"Come Kanani. You have grown bigger and stronger in these warm waters, so you are now ready to come with me on a wonderful journey. We will swim to a special place far away where we will find plenty of delicious food to eat."

"Can my friends come too?" asked Kanani.

Her mother smiled and Kumu the wise old goatfish shook his head and said

"No Kanani, we can't swim that far. But you will make new friends in the cold waters of the north, and when you have eaten enough food you must journey back and tell us all about your faraway friends. We will be eager to hear about your journey, so be sure to come back again." His beard wagged as he spoke.

"I'll be back" Kanani assured them.

The octopus, the turtle, the red squirrel fish and all her other friends gathered around to watch her go. They waved goodbye and with a swirl of her tail she was gone.

Ahead of them lay the big blue ocean, and Kanani wondered what sort of creatures they would meet on their journey.

They were joined by three friendly dolphins. With a splish and a splash the dolphins dove in and out the waves, leaving a wake of white foam behind them. Kanani's mother said

"These dolphins are your smallest cousins and on our journey we will meet more cousins. Some big, some small. Some nice and some mean. We all look different but we belong to the same family. The WHALE family."

They hadn't gone much further when a big dark shadow loomed above them. The shadow belonged to a creature who was so big – he seemed to blot out all the light coming from the sky above.

Kanani kept close to her mother but her mother told her not to be afraid of the big Blue Whale.

"He is your biggest cousin but he will not hurt you." The big Blue Whale swam quietly by.

Day after day Kanani and her mother swam and swam with nothing but each other and the wide open ocean for company. They only stopped to rest or for Kanani to drink from her mother.

The creamy milk tasted good and it made Kanani strong so she could swim a long way every day.

Once, while she was drinking, her mother said "Look over there, Kanani!" What was her mother looking at, Kanani wondered.

"Another baby whale with his mother!" Kanani exclaimed.

The baby whale was playing with his mother and Kanani laughed because she played the same games with *her* mother. "But why do they have all those big teeth?" she asked.

"Because they are Sperm Whales and Sperm Whales use their teeth to eat big creatures like squid and sharks. We don't have teeth because we don't need to bite or chew our food. We eat tiny creatures called krill, so all we do is swallow. It's nice and easy – you'll see."

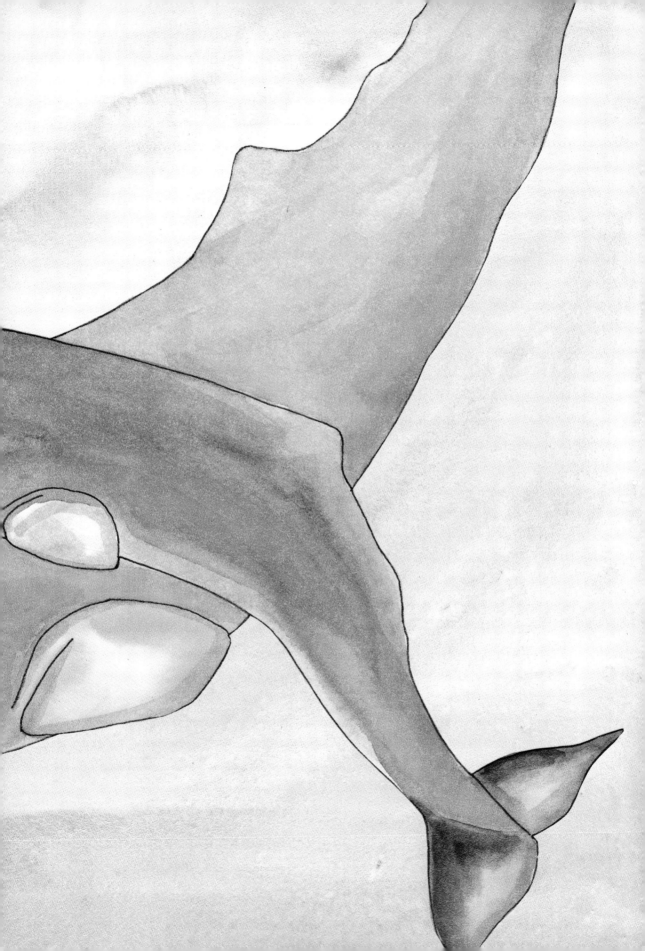

Later they swam alongside two creatures who were almost as long as Kanani's mother. They had friendly faces and their long bodies were covered with barnacles.

Kanani's mother told her that they were Gray Whales.

Suddenly one day Kanani's mother stopped and listened. She didn't like what she heard so she and Kanani swam away as fast as they could.

Speeding through the water were three black and white creatures. Their sharp pointed teeth frightened Kanani. She was glad that they were swimming away. When they were safe her mother said

"Those were Killer Whales, and they are mean if they are hungry. Killer Whales will sometimes attack a baby whale, and even when you are fully grown it is better to keep away from our fierce cousins."

On quiet days when they stopped to rest, there was nothing Kanani liked more than playing with her mother. Her mother was loving and patient and she always took such good care of Kanani.

Kanani loved leaping out of the ocean and splashing back onto the water. Sometimes if she was very sleepy she would lie on her mother's strong back. That way it was easy for her to stay above water so she could breathe.

As the days went by it got colder and colder, and one day Kanani saw lumps of white ice floating in the ocean.

Crash! Crash!

Kanani heard a loud cracking sound like thunderclaps.

"That is the sound Right Whales make when they are playing" said her mother. Kanani watched the Right Whales crashing and splashing about in the water. They were having such fun!

Kanani swam passed a big iceberg. Two small gray creatures dipped about in the water alongside her.

"Narwhals" said her mother and Kanani greeted her horned cousins as they swam gracefully by.

Suddenly the water was full of thousands of tiny orange creatures.

"Food!" cried her mother, and she opened her mouth. Her throat stretched as she swallowed an enormous mouthful of krill.

Kanani swallowed her first mouthful of krill. It was delicious.

"It's good to be here!" Kanani exclaimed. "We swam such a long way and we were so hungry, but now we can eat as much food as we like."

Kanani smiled as she looked around at her beautiful new home. The wise old goatfish was right. She would enjoy being here for a while. She would eat plenty of food and play with her new friends – but one day she would swim back to her warm water friends and tell them all about her wonderful journey.

The Wonderful Journey

Humpback Whales take approximately 80 days to swim from Hawaiian to Alaskan waters – a distance of 3 000 miles.

They breed offshore Hawaii and feed offshore Alaska, and during the 4–5 months spent around Hawaii the adult Humpbacks eat virtually nothing. When they reach their feeding grounds, an adult will eat more than one ton of krill in one day.